SAFTOR

AND

THE LIFE SOURCE

BY

COLIN. K. S.

HELLO, I AM ERON; I AM GOING TO SAY THE STORY OF MY LIFE TURNING UPSIDE DOWN FROM GETTING BULLIED IN SCHOOL TO HUNTING AND KILLING DEMONS. I KNOW IT SOUNDS WEIRD AND UNBELIEVABLE BUT, IT'S TRUE.

WELL AFTER HEARING THIS STORY YOU MIGHT WANT TO BE SOME MAGICAL HERO, WELL IF YOU ARE THINKING LIKE THAT QUIT THAT IDEA RIGHT NOW UNTIL YOU WANT YOUR WHOLE HAPPY LIFE RUINED. I PROMISE IT IS NOT FUN KILLING AND GETTING KILLED BY DIFFERENT FEROCIOUS MONSTERS AND ALSO DISCOVERING PAINFUL TRUTHS, GETTING BETRAYED AND OTHER HEROIC STUFFS.

WELL LIKE MOST OF THE OTHERS I HAD A NORMAL LIFE, BEFORE ... YOU KNOW, IT TOOK A U-TURN AND EVERYTHING CHANGED. FIRST I WILL START WITH MY BEFORE LIFE.

SO LET'S START THE STORY

JUST A MISERABLE DAY AT SCHOOL

In school I had a few friends but Evan was my best friend, he lives few houses far from my house. I was getting bullied almost daily in school; it was like I was the favorite victim of the bully Frag and his gang. He always tries to make me fall in the corridor by either pushing me from back or putting his leg in the way while I am walking, I mostly fall for it but sometimes I don't know how but my chest will be like afloat in the air while my leg is still in touch on the ground and suddenly comes back to normal position. Then Frag and his bully gang will be saying to me that it was just my luck and they will later try their pranks on me when they got me alone.

One day as usual I got up early, got ready and went to school on the usual school bus. I sat near Evan, who was willing to see me to say how wonderful the film they saw last night was. His explanation didn't even finish when we reached school which was only less than two kilometers from my home, but I have to go by bus because my parents were always busy and wanted to go to office early as well.

After Evan's long explanation about the movie the class started. The first period was usually science but today our science teacher was not feeling good, so today the first period was free until our math teacher showed up about half hour before the period ended and started teaching about one and half hour as second period was also math. We were already tired after the second period.

At lunch time when I was going to the table where Evan was sitting suddenly someone pushed me from the back and when I fell down, it hurt badly in my chest. Suddenly some energy flowed through my veins and I stood up and when I looked at who pushed me, it was Frag. I felt unusual anger and I shouted that I have had enough and suddenly I beat him so hard that his head hit the table nearby. And his friends surprised and scared ran away and Frag seeing them running away murmured "traitors". He tried to beat me, but I kicked him in the chest hard enough for him to go back hit a nearby pillar and fell down. He couldn't move and was also slowly moaning from pain. Suddenly the quick energy left my body and I were left in the middle of the mess with others staring and clapping at me. I took another meal and even the lady staff in the mess was appreciating me like I had just defeated a monster that was threatening them for years, which was kind of correct.

I then went and sat near Evan and started eating, he didn't even talk. After lunch up to evening nobody talked to much expect showing me thumbs up I was surprised that even a few teachers who had been teased by Frag smiled at me when I was going back to class from the mess room.

When school was over principal called me to his room and I to be honest was not surprised to see my parents and Frag and his Mom standing near the principals chair but I was surprised when Frag's mom gave me the you-did-good smile. The principal sat on his chair and he started to speak to my parents about what happened and they were like didn't mind cause I did it for my own protection and she also told about me complaining about Frag bullying me for years . Then Frag's mom started to speak and the thing I thought the least would happen, actually happened she said to smile "Well, I don't have a complaint, at last he deserved more than this." The principal , my parents and my four year older brother Dray who was standing in the corner whom I hadn't noticed until then and mostly me was surprised by this speech and even Frag himself started protesting with his own mom . His mother told him to shut up and say sorry to me for everything he had done or else he would get extra beats from her when they reached home. Frag thought it was better not to argue.

He mindlessly said sorry to me with a threatening and scared look in his face. His mom said to the principal "I allow not only this kid, I allow all teachers, staff and students to teach him a lesson if he does something wrong. He deserves it." The principal all confused from the unusual scenario said "That settles it, now all of you can go home." We left the school in car and nobody expect Dray seemed to talk about the incident. Dray told me that he was proud for having me as his brother. But then I saw a sudden sadness look on his and my parent's face when they hear him say that. I thought I must have imagined that and came back to the happiness of defeating the school bully without any problems.

Finally the end of the school year came and we all the students threw the English question papers in the air and rushed out with our friends. At that night we did nothing expect simply sitting in our rooms and making plans for the vacation , calling my friends and asking about their plans and just going down to eat dinner .

Brother's Call

One day I was sleeping in my bed peacefully as it was summer vacation. Suddenly my phone rang somewhere in the room completely destroying my peaceful sleep. I woke up and started looking around the whole room for my phone with sleepy eyes, I suddenly stepped on a wet cloth and slipped and fell down on my back. But then, I also found my phone under my bed, I must have left it there last night. I looked who was calling; it was my one and only brother Dray who was like four years older than me.

I answered the phone thinking why he is calling me this morning even when he was the next room. Dray spoke first, good morning Eron.

I replied in a sleepy but confused voice, why are you calling me when you are just the next room? He replied in a smiling voice, well you are in trouble young man.

"Today early morning principal called mom and said all of us to come to school for discussing something serious about you"

But also said to not bring you, But now mom said me to call you and to tell you to come to school ASAP.

Before I could reply Dray ended the call and I was left alone with confusion of why principal called her in the middle of the vacation, while he could have said it before the vacation started. I was starting to get scared as I thought that ,principal called mom to complaint about something related to me like my extremely bad progress in school ,as it is the only valid reason to call her in the middle of vacation, but I am pretty sure I did well . Anyway if that is the reason, I might get there soon before mom gets real mad.

So I got ready fast and when I looked around my room which was a little mess, so I cleaned it fast so that my mother won't be extra mad at me for that. Then I suddenly rushed outside locked the door , took my bicycle and started riding very fast to the school , when I got there , I saw my father's car and suddenly my fear increased like ten times .

I then parked my bicycle and started walking to the entrance but it was locked. So when I looked around I saw that the door to the hall was open. I then started to walk straight to the door slowly.

When I was walking towards it suddenly Dray comes out and sees me coming and then shouting something ran inside closing the door.

This made me think that I was going to get killed. I reached in front of the door and I put my hand on the handle and opened it,

All through the way from my home I forgot a very important thing that it was April 5th, my Birthday but the others didn't forget it.

The moment I opened the door I heard many pops and shouting Happy Birthday Eron. Behind the door was magnificent decoration all over the hall in front of me was my family and all my class mates, a big cake with decorations all around showing the number thirteen. It took a few moments for me to realize what is happening. Then suddenly they put birthday cap on my head and dragged me near the cake and then they started singing happy birthday and I fully relieved and moreover very happy started cutting the cake after that every one clapped and Evan my best friend came from the crowd and took a piece of the cake and decorated my face with it. Everyone and surprisingly I myself started laughing at this. Then we ate the cake, I had my face washed and we did many activities like singing, dancing, playing games, etc… At last the party was over I thanked everyone and me and my family started to go back to my house. I was in the car while Dray was riding the cycle back home.

At last when we arrived and opened the door they straightly took me to a non used room at upstairs and when I entered the room I saw a huge pile of gifts. My Father said from the back 'It's all your. '

But my mother said , you can unwrap them now , we will eat lunch after some hours as we have ate so much cake an all those food from your party . So go open them and don't forget to tell us what you have got.

I fully stunned cause of what happened because I first thought it was going to be bad day but it turned out to be the best. I then dashed to the presents and also asked Dray to help me out .The first one I opened was from Evan, it was a toy sword but a good one made out of light metal, with a snake or veins like design all over the blade with a very much decorated silver handle. I liked it so much that I decided to keep it safe and not to damage it. I got many good gifts and at last left was a sketchy pretty large box with a shining black wrapper with at the top was written on a paper which was stick to it written ' From Saftor - It's Your Time '

After seeing this Dray grabs it from me before I was able to unwrap it and he also said 'You better start cleaning this mess up or mom will be not happy anymore. ' Then Dray rushed down stairs to the kitchen where my parents were cooking.

He told them something showing the box, there was a fearful and surprised look in their faces and they discussed for some time and at last my father grabbed it from him and rushed to their room.

I was watching all of this from the top of the stairs but still I couldn't hear anything. I suddenly went back to the room and pretended to have seen nothing.

After some hours Dray called me down for lunch and I choose to not ask about the gift believing that it should be for my own good.

That Sketchy Present Returns

After Lunch I went to sleep for some time but at first I couldn't sleep thinking of that present, at last almost an hour later I finally got some rest. I slept until almost five in the evening when Dray woke me up and said we were going shopping to buy presents for me. I got ready soon.

We left home after six. We first went to a shop where I purchased many items like board games, toy sets , and we even bought a gaming console which I only had dreamed of which made it suspicious cause they wouldn't have bought a game console for me as my parents always said it was not good . We then went to the checkout, but when we were going back to the car I was talking and laughing and I was very happy until I got a feeling that someone was behind , watching me and when I looked back and there standing was a man wearing a big coat and a cap, as it was night, I didn't get to see his face but I could make out a small beard and in his left ring finger was a silver ring with a white stone in the middle , when I looked at my family they were already in the car and was telling me to get in.

I looked back once again but the man was gone, so I rushed back to the car and was about to tell them about the man but thought it was just my imagination and I decided to not tell them.

Then we went to buy us clothes in a nearby mall, we bought me many nice dresses, at almost eight at the night we went to a restaurant and bought pizza and went home, when we reached home it was quarter to ten. We changed dress and started eating. While we were eating I decided to tell them about the man and his appearance, the other three froze for a few moments and they told him that he might just be imagining it. After that conversation they didn't talk and ate fast and when finished eating and doing the dishes, mom told Dray and father that they needed to talk. And told me to go and sleep.

I thought this was suspicious but then came to a conclusion that it might be some family matters so I went to sleep. When I entered my room I found out that it was full of the presents and clothes that we just bought. So I took all of them and put it in an empty room and at last went to sleep.

Next morning I woke up early than usual and today was Sunday but my parents weren't fully free because they were busy workers in a big and famous electronic appliances company, they got breaks often but otherwise they were busy but always finds time to spend with us. Today was one of them days they were free.

After breakfast I rushed up and started to check out the items we bought yesterday night. But suddenly I noticed that there was a locket with the shape of a black nine tipped star with many designs on it that looked similar to the ring of the man I saw last night and with a purple gem like stone in the middle instead of white one like that man's ring, it plain gold back side, I ran downstairs and asked my father how it got there, he replied that I might have put in the cart to buy and I might have forgotten about it. I thought that was possible and I decided to wear it always as it looked very cool.

Suddenly my mom told that Evan has came to play with me, so I ran to the door and led Evan to upstairs to the room where all his presents were kept.

He was actually stunned when he saw this, He said "It looks like you have bought and entire section of a store." I Replied Yeah , but it's a little suspicious about the things happening here like my first birthday party at school , way more birthday presents , it seems a bit odd , and I also told him about the man I saw last night and the my locket which looked similar to the man's ring . After hearing this Evan said " Well you must be imagining things or even if the man is real , you both were near the same store , so he might have bought the ring from the same store as your locket . " In suddenly replied "Why haven't I thought about this, anyway I am going to need help arranging these and to play with these so won't you help me?" Evan replies smiling "Yeah, sure. Let's go. " We kept playing games on the console until lunch when Evan left.

That night mom suddenly says "We are going out to watch a film so get ready fast and don't forget to wear matching dress." So we got ready fast and went out to watch a film and also ate dinner from outside but when we returned, it was very night and everyone was tired so we went straight to sleep. I jumped on the bed but got up soon because the sharp point of the locket was stinging my chest, so I put it in the drawer and went to sleep without even changing clothes.

The whole week went peacefully, and I still hasn't seen the man again so I believed that it was just an imagination, until on the Saturday at like six in the morning I woke up to the sound of some people talking, I recognized those as the sound of Dray and my parents but after sometime I heard a deep and warm voice which I haven't heard before.

I woke up and slowly went to the top of the stairs but when I started coming down I was surprised to see the man I saw at that night sitting on the couch and Dray and my parents sitting on another couch opposite the man. I could hear dad asking in a sad voice "Should well him the truth now?" The man instantly replied " No, I will handle that you just do what I told you , I know it is hard you have did what they have asked you , but it's time , and you will see him again , I shall go now " And the man just walks out and just disappears . My parents and Dray were sad. So I, surprised of the man's appearance went back to my room silently and tried to sleep thinking it was just a dream after some time I woke up and brushed my teeth and bathed.

Dray suddenly enters my room and told me that breakfast was ready and to come down and eat.

When I reached down I thought all of that was a dream because they were acting like nothing happened. After finishing breakfast and washing my hands. I went back to my room and was surprised to find that the present which Dray took from me last week was lying on my bed with my locket beside it. Now

A sudden thought occurred to me that, this unknown present might be from that man. I closed the door and went near the box and took the locket and I wore it. I then took the box in my hands and it felt heavy. I tore the shiny black wrapper and there was a thin metal box with "Happy Birthday Eron" punched into it. I thought that "If the present is from the stranger how he knows about my birthday and why was he in my house and my parents were talking to him like they knew him." Without waiting much I opened it from the side and from it slid a rectangular box with super shiny gens and beads and on the top written in red gems 'Saftor' I was amazed by the beautiful box.

I opened it to find some strange looking sweets like a curly chocolate which acted like a spring and many chocolates with the figures of people and animals which looked like they were alive.

I was speechless by the present it looked like it cost so much money for the box itself and the chocolates are like magic. There were some more things other than the chocolate. One was a very small glass bottle with a shining blue liquid in it and the other one was a tin golden card with the number nine hundred ninety seven written on one side and the other side was written Saftor, I wondered what it was and then put in my pocket .Then I started eating the chocolate and in a hurry I ate so much and I felt like vomiting so I ran to the washroom and vomited, after cleaning up I came back. I then sat on the bed and I felt something cold near my hand , when I looked it was the small bottle, I took it in my hand and kept it in the box thinking if it is some kind of sweet juice I will drink it later , I don't want to vomit again soon ..

I then cleared the cover from the bed and took the box once again and put it on my lap I then opened it and took out the bottle and thinking it might be some kind of sweet syrup opened the bottle and drank it.

It tasted sweet a little sour but instead of cold it felt little warm after drinking it I felt very tired , my body started to lose strength and suddenly my whole body started disappearing into small particles and now I as nowhere to be seen in the room and all I could see was a dark and blank area . I thought it would rather be a poison or the overdose of sugar must be messing with my brain.

At Saftor, My Real Home

All I could see was darkness, until I saw few grey shining particles flying around and suddenly it formed a big grey shining circle above my head. The circle then disappeared and the outline of a room came into view. I saw a grey outline of a woman, a man standing near her with a baby in his hand. They were happy and were playing with the baby, but suddenly the house felt like shaking and they started panicking and the wall on one side of the room broke and something started to enter the room. Before I could see what it was it faded away and instantly I was falling down into darkness and suddenly with a thud I fell on something And it cracked , I didn't feel pain when I looked what I had fell on . I was shocked to see that it was a skeleton but not normal skeleton from the skull two big pointy sharp horns were there but suddenly the bottom of the horn started cracking and it broke and flew at a high speed to my eyes but before it hit me I felt something kicking hard on my chest and I fell back , but this time it was not skeletons but thin layer of water , I stood up and I was on the edge of a river and on the other side was a big banyan tree and in front of it was a small hill of its veins grown as if it is protecting something .

The vein endings on the top of the triangle hill started to go back like it's growth was reversed the after some time something bright shone on the top if the veins it was a golden sword handle , when I was looking at the sword handle . I felt coldness around my legs, when I looked down the water from the river was grabbing my feet and it suddenly pulled me into the river. Then I was thrown into darkness again but before long I opened my eyes.

First my vision was blurry and then it became clear. Actually I was freaked out when I suddenly saw the man I saw that night staring at me from the corner of an empty room expect a bed in the middle of the room with me lying on it and the man on the corner sitting on a wooden chair staring at me like I was going to be the victim of a murder case.

I thought it must be a dream and I pinched myself hardly on my hand I almost shouted AAh cause it hurt very much and I realized it was all real. The man stood up and started to walk straight to me. I shouted at me man if he had kidnapped me by giving me poison. I don't know what I was shouting but I was shouting random things. He without minding it came near me and he put his hand on my head and I instantly stopped shouting and I fell asleep.

When I woke up I was in the same room and the man was standing near my head but he changed his black costume and now was wearing shirt and pant like a normal person. He was about six feet tall and his hair was light brown and he had a small beard and moustache of the same color. His expression was calm. Before I could say anything he said to me in the same deep and warm voice to calm down and that I was not kidnapped or poisoned. He sat near me and apologized for making fearful entry.

I didn't know what to say and I was not sure if this was a dream or if it is real. He then started introducing himself "My name is Dolof, I am the current head and owner of Saftor house. From now onwards this is your home. If you are thinking it is a dream, it is not, all of this is real. " Now I understood who had sent me the unknown present. I confused stated asking multiple questions like whether this is really real, if he had poisoned and kidnapped me and when will I go back. I took a cup of boiling water and I think Dolof already knew what I was about to do and he looked at me with don't-do-it look and of course I didn't listen to him and poured a few of the boiling water to my left hand and shouted in pain .

After Dolof had caught the falling cup that slipped from my hand and had put some ice on the burnt spot, he told me to not do anymore stupid things. I had confirmed that this was real cause when I touched the burnt part in hurt really bad. He then told me to get sleep if I want or to go with him to see some things. I told him that I would come after sometime. He then left the room and I was still kind of confused but after processing what had happened right now I took a small nap. When I woke up I wished it was all a dream but when stood up I was in the same room but when I touched the burn mark it was not there I was confused again. Right then Dolof came in through the door. I told him about the mark's disappearance. He smilingly told me that it was the magic of this place "No injuries last forever in this place."

"Now if you will come with me, I shall introduce you the house and its rules and we shall also decide about your room."

I agreed and we left the room. What I saw out of the door was normal on top of the door that we just exited was written ' New comer's rest room ' and in front of the door was a small empty corridor without any other room and at the end of the corridor was another big door.

When we were walking I noticed that the walls were painted gold on grey with the designs of vines and animals and they were moving, the vines were growing and the animals were moving here and there in slow motion. When Dolof opened the big door he said "Welcome to your home brave palin." Out of the door was a small round corridor with handles on the side which I thought is necessary cause in the middle like ten floor below was a huge circular ground about half the size of a stadium, tiled with black and white tiles which reminded me of chess. All around it was many layers of floors like the one I was right now standing on.

I turned to Dolof in amazement and asked him what this place is exactly. Then he started walking and I followed him he started an explanation " This is Saftor House , owned by the Saftor family of which I am a member of that is why I said that I owned this place , anyway here we bring special children from the whole universe , by special I mean really special . From the creation of universe the whole species was divided to two major categories those are normal and magical. The magical human community was named Palins by the ancestors.

In Saftor these children are trained in both magical as well as normal ways to their maximum. You might think being magical is better but No! We can't live peacefully cause there is also bad side for even magic. There are many demons, creatures and monsters we have to face, that is why we are training these children so that they can live through the evilness and live happily. I think that would do the introduction. Now we shall see about your room."

I was surprised by what he said. That means magic is real and I might be one of them. I followed him to an empty and dark room, we entered and suddenly exited it and then I understood we were on the eleventh floor. We went through a couple more of those rooms and now we were on the fourteenth floor. We turned into a corner and after walking for a few seconds through the corridor we stopped and to my right was a sealed silver door with a silver knob and there was a card slot right under the know and on the door was written Nine Nine Seven and I understood I had to put the golden card I have got into that slot. Dolof also told me to do so.

The moment I put the card in the slot, the door started to grow vein designs from the slot where I had inserted the card and when it stopped, the veins started to glow cyan color and the color was spreading though out the door. When the color had finished spreading the whole door was made out of shining cyan colored metal which was actually my favorite color and when the door opened. Inside was a magnificent room with A good bed a door on the edge which I thought would be to the bathroom and there was even a T.V. and a gaming console connected to it and even a gaming pc on a desk, on another edge near to the wall was a big enough book shelf with many books which when I looked there was all types of books I liked to read and all my favorite books were also there. The whole room was cyan themed. The room was just perfectly like the room I always wanted.

Dolof standing outside the door told me to stay here and ready up my room and he will call me if there is any emergency and he left. I couldn't believe that I was standing in my dream room.

THE GOOD OLD PROPHECY

I looked around the whole room and I recognized that the room was quite big and there was an open show case on the wall with many collectible items of super heroes and other fictional people. There was a cupboard near the wall in which when I opened were many playing and sports items like tennis bats , football , chess and many more . Only after some time did I realize that there was a couple of luggage near my bed.

When I opened them I thought they were my old stuff from my home. But I was wrong, they were brand new clothes in one big luggage and those clothes were also super hero themed which I liked most wearing at home. In the other small luggage was what I thought few set of uniforms cause it was printed on them Saftor. I thought what these were for because I haven't seen anyone wearing them when I was walking by. Then I noticed a paper on the side of the luggage. It was written 'This uniform is not for daily use this is only for special days such as tournaments and parties. ' I wondered if there is tournaments and parties here.

Then I heard a knock on the door, when I looked it was Dolof, he told me that lunch will be served at one pm, and also that after lunch we needed to talk. I thought where I should go to eat lunch; maybe someone will come and call me. I looked around the room to find where I should keep these clothes then out of nowhere another cupboard appeared near the sport's cupboard. I arranged the clothes nicely and when I looked back at the luggage the bags suddenly disappeared, I thought that would have spared me sometime.

Then I went to the computer and after starting the computer I was surprised to see that all my accounts and files were in the computer and it had a very strong internet connection which I later figured out was magic as I couldn't find any devices nearby . The case was same for the gaming console also all my games were already there. After playing games for some while suddenly I heard another knock on the door. I thought it might be someone who came to take me to the mess hall so I turned of everything and when I opened the door , I was mistaken again it was a lady pushing a food trolley into my room .

I asked the women if we are always eating in our own room. She replied "No dear, this is only for new comers. You will be able to eat with your new friends once your formalities are complete." I understood what she said and I thanked her for bringing me food which was nice of me. The lady then exited and said me to keep everything on the trolley after eating and to press the button on the side of the trolley after I was done. I looked around and found a green switch on the side of the trolley. I started to eat; there were many kinds of dishes like fried chicken, ice cream, pastries and more. After I finished eating and washing my hands, I did as the lady told me. I kept the plates and wastes on the trolley and pressed the green button and suddenly the trolley just disappeared. I looked on my white bed and there were many stains on it but when I tried to clean. It suddenly changed to dust particles and flew away.

Then I remembered that Dolof wanted to talk to me so I waited for him and within few minutes he came. I followed him to the nearest 'dark elevator' which is what I named the dark rooms because I didn't know what else to call them. When we entered the room Dolof told me to think 'Floor number one.' So I did so and when we exited we were not one floor below but now we directly went to the first floor.

We went through a couple of corridors and we finally arrived in front of a thick golden door but this door had many designs related to nature. The moment Dolof put his hand on the door it opened. Behind the door was a huge and massive room with much furniture, book shelves and other items. In the middle of the massive room was a big glass chamber in which was a beautiful tree which looked very healthy. Another noticeable thing was a big ball of golden particles flying in the air at one end of the office. Dolof went near it and he raise his hand and the particles separated to reveal a shining white scroll it slowly flew down to his hands and Dolof told me to come and sit next to him in a chair. He told me with a serious look on his face to me that "What you are about to hear is very important, so listen carefully ."

He raised the scroll in the air and suddenly it flew from his hand into the particles again but this time started to glow brightly and I heard a tick male voice speaking. "The darkness of evil is for eternity but at any cost they should be kept under control, all beings have the power to fight against evilness but only a chosen one will be able to defeat it. The one and only chosen one will be born by now, but he can only fight them after he is awakening."

I know you hadn't understood anything now, but you will get it eventually. But let me say this hope of the whole universe lies on this prophecy. The chosen one mentioned here can be anywhere in this house or will come to this house or there is a chance it might be you. I was stunned by his speech but I spoke "Anyway, what is the point." Dolof came to his normal face again he told " The point is that there is a test in here which might have a chance in finding the chosen one and might even can awaken him or her , so I wanted you to know this and also the fact that your chance for the test will be coming soon . This process will make him or her so strong that he or she can take down demons on their own. "

I only understood a few things and I still had many doubts to ask but I chose to ask a question that I wanted to ask ever since I have got her. "What is so special about me that bought me here?"

Suddenly his face went into a sad expression that I had never seen him in before and he looked at me as if he had no other option but to tell me. He told me to come along with him to his main table.

My True Identity

When we sat near the table Dolof took out two files which I recognized as children's file in which all the information about them were written Andrew Macson and Stelli Homus . Who are these I asked confused.

These are your real parents

I have almost forgotten about my family cause of everything happening here. But when I heard this I was shocked and I couldn't just believe that.

What, No I have never seen these two people and I was with my family always as I remember.

Dolof was now trying his best to convince me about it. Me I can't just think that these two people whom I had never seen as I remember and I can't just think that all the days I lived until now not knowing who my real parents were I thought this was just a joke cause I have seen Dolof going around the house playing and joking with children .But I don't think that he will joke about this much sensitive topics.

Dolof started speaking .When you were seven months old, after hearing the prophecy, he king demon of that time and now name Tyrone came to your house to kill you thinking that you might be the one said in the prophecy. but your parents fought him but he was too strong for them to defeat him so they decided to sent you safely to earth, to a family they knew and trusted to keep you safe, that is the family that you have been living ever since and your parents have told them to not tell you anything at all until it's time.

I was speechless because the people I thought was my family never told me this. Tears were flowing from my eyes and I asked one final question, but when I asked my voice was chocked with sadness.

Where are they?

Well, nobody knows ever since then. Maybe they are hiding .

I was so sad and angry that I jumped from the chair and without thinking anything else ran to my room even though I was not sure where my room was but when I closed my eyes for one second and opened it, I was inside my room .

At the office Dolof was amazed by what I did .and he immediately pressed a bell on his table and a staff member came running through the door. Dolof told him to get the arrangements for the test by next week.

In my room I was crying for many time and it took me hours to relax and to accept the truth. From the next day onwards my excitement about the place was way less but after the day . I somehow recovered and tried to forget what I have heard . Dolof always kept a look on me just to make sure I was okay .

Within a few days I forgot about that even if not completely. Whenever I try to sleep the image of my parents getting attacked by the demon comes to my mind.

After a week my clothes started to become smelly so I did a small research and found out that we needed to bring the clothes to a specific room at the house and give them to a couple of workers who will be there or you can do it by yourself it is simple just throw the clothes into a pool of water in the room and suddenly they will start to spin around and will fly out of the water and automatically dry instantly and the will come back into your arms folded. This is very fun to watch.

Within some days I had made many new friends, every time I see them it reminded me of Evan. The best friend I made was girl named Elisa who had always been nice to me from the moment we met. She was the same age as me. She was about an inch shorter than me. She had copper blonde hair. She showed me many things about the house and about the events happening here. Overall we were very good friends. But I still miss Evan so much.

One day I was returning to my room after washing clothes and entered my room. I kept the clothes in my cupboard . Suddenly Dolof entered the room and told me that my test is about to begin.

I followed him to his office and we entered the office, there was nothing new in that office then I noticed another Door in his room and we went through it and there was several doors on either side of the small corridor we were walking through and at the end of the corridor was a small Hall like room with a door on the other side which you can confirm from just seeing it was at least a three feet thick metallic door , I got this feeling that it was for something very dangerous and very powerful .

I hadn't had a chance to ask him about how this is done. So I asked him and he turned to me and said

That room right there is made up of kolminan the strongest magical metal invented till now and it is also protected by many powerful spells casted by the most powerful palins that we know. Most importantly that room is filled with demon skin of two demons named Handelina and her twin brother Finor. Do you know what is so special about them?

No

Well they were one of the most feared king demons of all time cause they kept killing innocent people in huge numbers and one day some of the powerful warriors decided to put a stop to it and they did, but also found out that all demon's head, heart or skin held their special power and this body part will remain un harmed even after the demon is dead and the rest of the demon is reduced to nothingness. They found out that in the case of Handelina and Finor, it was their skin which had the power to remind people of all the times they met Demons even though this made them scared and weak in many people this made them angry and thirsty for revenge and this made them powerful.

Thankfully, this time I was listening carefully and I understood what he meant. He is going to put me in that room and reminding me of the times I had met demons and if the miracle happens and I am the chosen one something big will happen.

Dolof asked the two people standing near the door to open it. They people I recognized as guards put their hand on the door and suddenly their hands were twice as big as a normal man they were like, they had super strength but still they struggled very much to open the door and when they have opened it enough for me to go through I knew I was correct, the door was almost three feet thick. Dolof told me to go through and I looked at him for one last time like I was going to surely die in there and walked inside the room and all I saw was darkness and suddenly they closed door and I heard Dolof shouting me good luck which was the last thing I heard and the tiny gaps between the doors through which tiny rays of light was coming suddenly sealed.

I was standing in the darkness without knowing what to do suddenly many things started to glow around me in fire blue and orange colors when I tried to move away from them I realized I was floating in the air with tiny shining blue and orange particles all around me and in the next moment I was flying in the air and the particles disappeared, I thought I might fall down but I didn't. Then I saw small rope like projections coming from the scales and when they got near they grabbed me around my waist, hands, legs and my neck and many other similar ropes shot at me in the speed of light and I screamed in pain and I can't open my eyes and suddenly the pain stopped and I opened my eyes just to see the same dream again that I saw every night but this time it was clear and I was standing inside the room with them I realized that the couples were looking almost same to the pictures I saw on the student files and I knew they were my parents and I was the baby in their hand .

I tried to move closer to them but I can't move and when I looked I had no body. Suddenly I heard the wall cracking and a demon I recognized as Tyrone as Dolof has said about him but this time I recognized that he was bigger that I thought he was made out of black stone and blue fire was burning through the cracks and his head had horns pointing towards the side. In his hand was a sword which looked familiar with its master as it was also made out of black stone and Blue Fire but had some inscriptions on it. He then instantly transformed into a normal good looking man but then suddenly his horns came back but smaller and from the end of his lips were cracks with blue fire burning in them and his eyes was pure blue fire . He told them to give him the baby that is me, but my parents refused and they took out a sword and started fighting the demon with me in one hand and suddenly a teen girl came running through the door and was scared and surprised to see the demon and she started to run into the demon as if to fight but my father stopped her and said something. My father gave me to the girl and told her something like to runway, at first the girl refused but her mother told her to go and everything will be okay, the girl sadly ran away crying. My parents kept fighting the demon and suddenly he pushed them back flying and they screamed and this made me so angry and sad that I tried to hit the demon but I can't and suddenly the demon started walking towards them who were lying on the floor but before I could see anymore the dream faded away and all I could see was darkness.

In the room I was in the air unconscious. Suddenly the ropes started to turn into ash and black blood started pouring down from my skin and suddenly a big shield like aura made out of fire forms around me and there is something written on the aura in patterns and some ancient language . My t-shirt started to burn and became ash and from my chest demon blood was flowing all over. My hair started to change into dark blue. My body started to become in a good physical shape. I opened my eyes and they were flaming orange. The aura around me started to behave like it was angry and it suddenly blasted and the kolminan all over the room and the door and even the spells broke like a crispy piece of chip.

Outside the room Dolof and the other guards luckily escaped the flying pieces of kolminan cause of the shield they have created. They all were happy because they have found the one they have been looking for years but they were also sad about the wreckage.

I was lying inside the room unconscious with black blood or demon blood as known to the palins.

THE HOPEFUL CELEBRATION

Dolof and the guards were lying on the floor unconscious and suddenly Dolof became conscious and stood up. He walked slowly and carefully through the wreckage and tried his best not to get his leg injured from the flaming hot kolminan. He then casted a spell and light was all over the room and all the wreckage was moved to a corner of the room.

He slowly walked to a black figure that is me lying in the middle of the room and when he looked around the entire demon scales where burnt to nothing. He came near me lying unconscious on the ground and said

Finally you came to save us.

I not knowing what happened was lying unconscious on the floor. Dolof then called the guard and told them to take me to the special medical room. They stood up fast and casted some spell and they took me to the medical room. Dolof then ran to his room and took out something like a microphone and spoke

There will be and immediate meeting. All children staff and everyone should be in the hall within half an hour. He then ran to hall.

I was lying unconscious in the medical room and I opened my eyes and saw Dolof sitting next to me drinking some hot drink. I looked at my own body and found out that my body was buff and on my chest was a circle like pattern with many lines and an ancient language which I have seen a couple of times somewhere. But when I gained full consciousness the symbol faded away and I had a sudden pain all over my body and I felt like my eyes were burning but all the pain stopped within ten seconds. Dolof was looking at me and smiling like nothing abnormal happened. Before I could ask anything. He gave me a shake hand and said "Congratulations Eron, for being the lucky and unlucky one." I felt for a moment that he was mocking me. Then he told me what had happened and who I really am now.

It was hard for me to believe it because I just came here almost a couple weeks ago and now I am the savior of this place. He also told me to take rest the whole day tomorrow will be a fun day.

I was not in the condition to think anymore until I had the thought that I will be able to take revenge of Tyrone for hurting my parents at last. Then I slept comfortably.

The next Dolof woke me up and told me to get freshen up fast and we had a party to attend. When I heard party , I thought it must be the parties that Elisa told me about, so I got up fast , ran to my room but as always I don't know where to go and as it happened last time it was like I teleported to my room in a blink . I freshened up and before I could open the door to get out I remembered I hadn't combed my hair, so I went to the mirror and I almost screamed when I say a dark blue haired and flaming orange boy standing in the mirror, I hit my face to make sure it was me and the image in the mirror also followed, then I realized it must be the effect of the test so then I combed my hair in my usual favorite style. When I looked in the mirror I was all blue – my dress, my hair and even my watch. Then I noticed my eyes doesn't match the color so I wished in my mind that it would have been cool if my eyes were light blue, the moment I said that in my mind my eye color changed to the perfect light blue color that I wanted.

'Whoa! That I have to admit is a cool super power. '

Then I exited the room and Dolof was already waiting for me outside in his best dress as I have seen. A white shirt with a handless brown leather jacket on the shirt and a brown leather pant similar to the jacket. He now looked even younger, even though he is like thirty five or something.

When we were at the big door, outside of which is the great hall. Dolof said

After the celebration is over and when the go-to-your-room bell rings come to my office, we have something very urgent to discuss.

Dolof opened the door and suddenly there was a huge cheering voice like the one we hear during football matches. Dolof raised his hands and suddenly the crowd was silent. Dolof told me to stay here until he calls me. He then walked towards the handle and started speaking in so loud sound that even if I was standing out of the building I could hear clearly.

'Today was the day we have been waiting for almost a decade and finally our hero has come to the game. Today we are celebrating to honor our hero. '

In the back of the door I was getting super nervous cause I have never been on stage that to with hundreds of audiences. Suddenly Dolof clapped his hand and all the walls and rooms around the hall expect the small area I and Dolof was standing disappeared into golden particles and I was like 'Oh, Great ' When I saw the whole crowd who were standing outside the building whom I realized were the remaining Palins from their villages. I was fully nervous with almost hundred audiences whom all I was seeing almost daily and now it was like thousands of people outside and I realized they were only from the nearest village because there was more than billions of palins in this universe. Dolof continued speaking like nobody new was there.

'I present to you our hero Eron '

There was the sound of clapping, cheering and shouting which was like the sound of lightning. Dolof dragged me near him and the sound increased. When they were silent again some people from the crowd shouted

What is the proof that he is the so called hero?

I was even more embarrassed with this and suddenly somebody from the crowd said something that they shouldn't have.

He is just like his father and mother, complete fools.

After hearing this all the embarrassment and nervousness went away and anger was boiling inside me and me and if found the person who had said it. It was a tall and bully looking boy named Phil whom I had seen bullying others before. He was the oldest child in the house. My vision was focusing on him only and suddenly my well combed hairs started to get messy and there was small electric currents here and there in my hair and instead of my blue eyes was electricity and my right fist was curled tightly and it was like made up of electricity. The anger inside me was increasing beyond the limit and Dolof was like expecting this he just said 'Uh – oh' and backed away all the audience was surprised and all backed away expect the bully who was still standing there looking at me amazed. I said in a murderous and powerful voice.

'You shouldn't have said that, now you will get bullied.'

Now I was floating in the air. He was stunned and didn't knew what to do and all the others were like encouraging me and I was surprised to see that even Dolof and other staffs were standing silently and watching.

I shot at him and he let out a huge scream and he tried to block my attack using his fire power and made a shield , which was of no use cause I went through it like it never existed and I punched him in the chest which reminded me of the fight between me and Frag the school Bully.

The boy flew into the air and hit the ground and was unable to stand or talk. All around me the children cheered as if they were waiting for this moment. I was no longer angry and my hair, eyes and hands were back to normal, but I was still flying, As I was no longer angry it took me a few seconds to realize what had happened then I realized I was flying and I was happy to find out that I can fly and amazingly looked at myself. I then flew to Dolof and then I remembered that what I did was not good. But Dolof was standing there calmly like nothing happened. When I looked down Phil was already taken to the medical room. Then Dolof came forward again and said

'Well, there you have the proof. '

Let the celebration begin.

Just after Dolof had said this the floor below us also vanished and we fell down but suddenly I used my flying power but Dolof was already down safely.

I went down and all the children lifted me in the air and took me to the place where all the food was kept. The stuffed my mouth with food and after I had somehow swallowed it many children started asking me questions like how did I do that and can I do this, can I do that and many other questions.

The party was great and many people congratulated me but most of them were for beating Phil.

We had so much fun and games but after some hours the bell rang and all the people went back to their homes and the disappeared building reappeared and I was also about to go to my room when I remembered to go to Dolof's office. So I ran to his office.

MY BUCKET LIST

I got lost a couple times but I still somehow made it to his office and only when I reached his office did I remember I could have teleported here the whole time. When I entered the room to be honest I was a little surprised to see Elisa sitting on a chair near Dolof.

He welcomed me in and told me to sit on the chair next to Elisa. I sat down.

Before Dolof started to speak, Elisa interrupted.

Nice job, for you-know-what, and also on beating up Phil, He was a trouble maker ever since he got here. I was looking for a chance to take my revenge on him for pouring milk on my hair. But anyway I think I will adjust.

Umm, thanks, I guess.

Dolof did a fake cough like the one you do to get attention. So can I start speaking?

Yeah, of course. She said and I think she might have blushed a little.

Ok, so I called you here to say some very important things. First of all Eron , you were like a guest of this house for this much days , so from tomorrow morning onwards you will have to do all things a normal student here does. That means you can start practicing from tomorrow onwards.

To be honest A small part of my mind was not ready to leave the hospitality, but I figured out I had no choice.

'Ok, so that means I can go to the mess and eat with my new friend's right?'

Yes, you can eat with your new friends as well as an old friend.

What, what do you mean.

Well you will figure it out soon but let me say this. Now that you are our hope of becoming free from Tyrone you are going to need special training. And our head leader here Elisa will help you with your training.

I was surprised by what he just said about Elisa. "What, you are the head leader here. You never told me that. When you were explaining about the whole house."

Dolof interrupted. 'Wait, what did she become friends with you when you just came here?'

Yes, kind of

Well, that is strange. She hardly ever makes friends with new comers or even others. And as I remember she does not make friends with boys at all.

Elisa was just simply sitting in the chair like nothing was happening.

Anyway Eron, What I wanted to say was after about three weeks of training you will have to go on a quest and also battle Tyrone. So train hard.

This caught Elisa's attention. She asked Dolof in an almost pleading voice whether she can go with me on the quest. But Dolof denied.

Now her voice was mixed with anger and sadness. 'This is so unfair. I have been here for years and I even haven't got a single quest or mission at all. And now you are giving him who just came here a couple of weeks ago a quest? '

Well, sorry dear I can't do anything.

Elisa stood up from her chair and ran out wards.

Dolof looked back at me well; sorry about that she is like that sometimes. She gets very much angry and upset if others get what she wanted. But another thing I wanted to show you was something you are going to like. Just turn around.

My Good Friend Returns

When I turned around, there was a blast of surprise and happiness in my mind. A familiar boy standing near the door, about my age was Evan. All I could think was this was not real. There is no way he is a Palin.

What are you doing here!

Well, you know you are not the only Palin in your neighborhood. Evan replied in his usual smile.

Believe it or not it was fully real. That explains the mysterious things happening in his house like things floating here and there sometimes and even the fire starting on its own but I thought all of this was my imagination.

I stood up from my chair and ran towards and I hugged him. I was not sure whether it was him or me or both of us who blushed.

I missed you man. Why didn't you tell me about this?

Well, this was for your own safety.

I looked back at Dolof but he was gone. Then Evan asked me to come to his room. Actually I have never been to any other student's room.

We were walking through a corridor when I realized we were walking towards my room, but before I could ask him we stopped in front of the room just the left side of mine. Room no. Nine hundred ninety six.

Whoa! Is this your room?

Yeah!

No way, you are just the next room of me.

What. Is your room nine nine seven.

Yes

Good, we can sneak into each other's room at night,

Wait, is that allowed here.

Well probably no but it doesn't matter until you are caught. Well before it gets really dark better go to your room. We will talk tomorrow.

Ok

When I entered my room and closed the door. There was sudden zip sound and when I looked around there was a new window like hole in the left wall and when I looked carefully it read Evan Murphy wants to meet you, do you want to allow him to meet you ? I was just stunned when I saw this. I have heard about this from many people especially Elisa, but I have not given much attention. But as I remember I just have to think about and I did so. Suddenly the framing around the glass turned into silver and now it was like I could see him clearly. He spoke first.

Well before you are confused this is called Versian Message. Just like your video call.

Wow! I thought it was fake.

Well, it's not and I just wanted you to know about it. So Good Night.

Good night.

I went to sleep soon without thinking about what just happened because I was super tired.

THE DAILY ROUTINE

The next morning was different. I woke up early and Evan was standing near my bed and when I looked what time is it. It was only six in the morning. I asked him why he woke me up.

Did you forget that from today you are going to follow the Daily Routine?

Oh Yeah, I almost Forgot.

He helped me stand up and told me to get ready soon and he will be back within five minutes. I sat some time because I was so sleepy then when I felt a little refreshed I went to the cupboard and looked for what dress to wear. Then did I only realize that the inside of the whole cupboard was different from what I had arranged. There were about seven sections with different dresses and all of the sections were named like Special uniform, Fight training Uniform, Free Time Dress, etc... I was confused which to wear now then I saw a section named Training Uniform I took out one of them and it was just a cloak that is about my Size. It was cotton and it's edges were light blonde color and the remaining was just light brown, it was just a simple cloak without much designs expect There was a stitching about at the chest level which read

Saftor and at the back side of the cloak was written my name in big bold letters ' ERON ' and it was a good cloak but I wondered how we were going to train with this but anyway I didn't have much time so I kept it on the bed and went to get ready after I came from bath. I tried on the Cloak. It was pretty heavy and it reached out to my toe which made it a bit hard to walk. But after a few seconds the cloak started to shrink and it edges met and it was like as if they were stitching themselves and with the next minute I was in real comfortable dress instead of the cloak I was wearing light brown T - Shirt and blonde pants. And in my T – Shirt was the same designs as the Cloak, A *Saftor* design and my name on the back. Then suddenly I heard a knock on the door.

Can I come in?

Yeah come in.

It was Evan he was also wearing the same dress as me expect instead of my name it was his name. He came near me and said "You look good in that dress."

Thanks

Do you mind me looking around the room? The training is not until seven so.

Yeah of course no problem.

He started looking around the room and examining the toys and other stuff after about ten minutes he came towards me and gave me a paper scroll which I didn't understand what it was until he told me it was the timetable. It was like –

7:00 am to 8:00 am - Training

8:15 am to 9:00 am – Yum ! Breakfast

9:00 am to 12:00 pm – Oh Man ! More training

12:00 pm to 1:15 pm – Oh Thanks ! Free Time

1:30 pm to 2: 30 – Lunch

2:30 pm to 4:00 pm – Yippee ! More Free Time

4:00 pm to 6:00 pm – Yess! Play Time

6:00 pm to 6:30 pm – You Smell ! Go Freshen Up

6:30 pm to 9:30 pm - Lets Go ! Entertainment

9:30 pm to 10:30 pm – Dinner

10:30 pm - Go Sleep

Wow, that is one long list. I told him after seeing it.

Yep, every day is a long day. He replied.

Can you explain what does this all mean?

Oh Ok, Well you there is total four hours of training and each hour it is different topics. And the four topics are physical training like sword fighting and other things then the next is magical items training in which you will study to take care of magical items then the next one is magical creatures in which you will obviously learn about and sometimes with magical creatures and I just wanted you to know sometimes rarely like very very rarely the creature get very attached to a child and the magical government and the house will allow them to keep it as a pet but that hasn't happened in many years and nobody here now is anyone like that but almost all people want one and honestly I would really like a dragon as a pet.

What, did you just say that dragons are real?

Yeah but not the ones that you see in movies they are looking almost the same but there are many differences also.

Oh, that is so cool; anyway continue what you were saying.

Ok, the last subject is pretty interesting. It's about learning legends, myths and histories of places, creatures and people. Well in free time you are allowed to go to your room or to the library or to wash clothes and other activities, but you are not allowed outside the building until playtime.

Ok so what do we play during play time? I asked with a little too much excitement in my voice.

Well, He replied. There are countless things to do. You can just roam around the garden or play any sports you like, you can also play chess with your friends outside or read books or listen to music, and there are many things to do. Now the best part. The entertainment. It is the my favorite time of the day cause then we will usually start with any announcements if there is any and then we will do many things like sometimes watch interesting movies, have a sing along or some good story tellers will narrate a story and mostly it is ghost stories or some interesting legends that we do not study in the training and if the staffs are in good mood they will arrange a camp fire. Then you eat dinner and go to sleep and you call it a day.

Wow, this place is so cool. I told him as if I am dreaming.

He suddenly looked outside the room and some children were already going to the training. So he told me to come. I followed him out the room and the door slammed behind me.

I ALMOST KILLED ANOTHER GUY

We ran towards the hall and in the hall the party decorations have been completely removed. All children were lined up in front of a small stage at the far side of the hall. We were at the back of the line until one of the staffs came and took us to the side of the stage. We stood there until Dolof entered the stage and greeted everyone good morning and started to tell them "Today onwards our new friend and you-know-who Eron will be starting his practice with you and I welcome him to the stage."

The staff that was standing behind me pushed me towards the stage with an expression like 'Better go there or I will stab you in the back. ' I went to the stage and there was a broke of applause. Dolof pulled me in front of him and put his hands on my shoulder and announced.

'I wish all of you would be nice to him.' When he said this I noticed that he was staring at a few children at the right bottom corner who were not at all in order and I realized them as Phil's best friends. Dolof continued his speech.

"Or else I fear they will end up in the same state as our so called Bully-baby." This caught everyone's attention and even the Phil's friends looked at me with disgust and anger. I have heard many people calling Phil many names like Bully-baby and when Dolof said this I understood that even the fully friendly headmaster hates him so much and to my surprise when he said this there was an even louder applause from the crowd and I noticed that even the staffs and teachers have joined and Dolof was smiling. Then he raised his hands as if telling everybody to shut up and they stopped the noise. I could see everyone looking at me hopefully and encouragingly expect of course the bully gang.

Dolof then told me I can go back to my place. So I ran down the stage as fast as I can because I am not that good on stages. When I was going back to Evan the children from Phil's gang made a threatening face at me as I was passing them. When the assembly was over we went to the sword training area outside and to be true it was the first time I have been outside the huge building in weeks. The outside was the most beautiful place I have ever seen in my whole trash life. There were lush green mountains more than a dozen of them all around the building which itself was on the highest and biggest mountain in the area and at the edge was a slope downwards towards the bottom of the other mountains. We marched towards the other side of the mountain where there was a huge ground about ten times bigger than the great hall and there were many sections like one section for archery , next one for sword fighting, another for running laps or so and many more. Evan suddenly came from my back and told me to come with him to swords training ground and when I asked what we are supposed to do here right now? He told me that we can do any type of training we like but the only catch is if we don't try everything we will just fail in the tests. My whole happiness and good mood was decreased when I heard that there is test here. When we entered the sword training area he took me to a shed nearby and in there was a huge and endless display of swords, double ended swords, spears and many more. Even if the cabin is small from the outside it is almost endless in the inside cause of the magic. We were looking for the perfect sword for me but none of them felt comfortable enough but we ended up choosing one that felt almost comfortable. Evan told me that it is hard to find the best sword so I have to adjust with it. I agreed because I knew I was not going to be good in it anyway. Then Elisa came in and I have not seen her since yesterday when she stormed off to her room but she looked very much happy and looked as gorgeous as always. She came near us and told Evan something and they told they will be back soon and told me that I can start practicing until they come.

First of all I hate it so much when people are ignoring me especially when I am just in front of them. Then they ran out the cabin and ran towards the entrance of the house and when I got out , I went to a dummy which was free while others were getting chopped down by other kids and I somehow lifted the sword and I was hitting the dummy with the sword like it will explode if I hit it hard.

Then I heard someone, no some people saying behind me "He can't even lift the sword properly. Do you remember the story of how his father was almost killed by Phil's father? He is just like his father, just show off. " I knew it was Phil's gang because I was expecting them to hit me anytime but I wasn't expecting them to repeat what Phil had.

This time things might have gone out of control cause last time I only wanted to hurt Phil but this time I really wanted to kill his whole gang. I had a sudden surge of anger and without thinking anything I flew the sword at the dummy and it was cleanly cut in half and then I realized inside of the dummy was pure metal and I have even cut through it. Even I was surprised but it didn't last long cause of my anger. But the children and even the mentors all around backed away. Phil's friends were also surprised for sometime but then they looked at me with a teasing expression. Then one of them whom I thought was the eldest of them all came forward as if to beat me in the face but when I raised my sword , it's blade was full Phil's friends were also surprised for sometime but then they looked at me with a teasing expression. Then one of them whom I thought was the eldest of them all came forward as if to beat me in the face but when I raised my sword , it's blade was fully damaged and only the handle survived without any damage. Before he could attack me one of the staffs whom I recognized as Dolof's assistant came running and told them to stop or else they will have to do the cleaning for the whole year.

There was a disappointing look in their face when they walked away. Then all of the other children went back to their normal training and the mentors went back to their job.

Then suddenly Evan and Elisa came running towards me and when they stopped they took some time to breathe then Evan told to me in a hurry voice.

"Maybe I am wrong; we will be going outside to get you a good weapon."

Then Elisa interrupted. I will be coming too.

I was pretty happy because my current sword is no more a sword because its blade is not even enough to cut an apple.

I GET SWALLOWED BY A RIVER

I asked them when should we leave and they replied. "You, I mean we want to go right now. Maybe after a few minutes. " We sat down for some time. Elisa started speaking to me like a councilor. "Well I think you have a temper problem."

Well. How do you want me to act when I find out that I am a magician and my life is doomed?

Well you have got a point. Elisa said this as if remembering a bad memory.

I changed the subject. When are we going to buy me a new sword?

Evan instantly replied. Buy?

Yeah, you said we are going to buy me a new sword.

Well, we are going on a quest to get you weapon. Like the most powerful weapon ever.

What. I replied full of confusion.

But this time it was Elisa who replied. I think you don't know about the sacred sword. Well, it is a legend that there is a sacred sword. Which are the most powerful weapon ever and it is said that the sword is said to be able to morph into any weapon and has the ability to kill any monster within seconds. But this sword is said to be waiting to be retrieved by a true hero who will one day take the fate of the whole universe in his hands.

Suddenly I remembered reading some story like this when I was going through the books in the library. Then after I have processed the story I asked them how we were going to find this sword or morphing weapon or whatever.

When I asked this. The smiled at me which made me a little uncomfortable. Then Elisa told me with a wicked smile that I was the key.

I thought this was possible because now I was like the big guy here. Then they both stood up and told me to go to my room and get whatever I want then we will be going. I just went with them so that I can change my disgusting look with sweat and dirt all over my face even if it was only a few minutes after the training having started. When I was about to enter my room I found out that Elisa was just the next room in nine nine eight. That means both my best friends are on my either side, this thought made me happy. I got in and washed my face and hands but I didn't change the training dress because I was comfortable in it.

B   When I exited the room both of them were already waiting for me. Evan was ready with a sword, a bow and a quiver full of arrows. Elisa was ready with a sword and a familiar book which I realized is the book in which I read about the legend of the sword.

I thought we might go to Dolof before we leave but we simply walked out the main gate and stopped in front of the gate. Elisa handed me the book and told me to navigate. I wanted to argue but suddenly I felt that they were right and I started going through the book when I suddenly stopped on a page with the image of a sword with a silver handle and a banyan tree behind it with a river flowing in front of it. Suddenly I remembered my dream and told them about it. They looked at me for a few seconds then they told me to just close my eyes and concentrate on the dream very hard. I didn't argue and I was trying to remember about the dream and suddenly I felt like a energy released from my hand and when I opened my eyes both of my friends were staring at something in my hand. When I looked down I realized I was holding a shining white orb made out of light itself. I tried moving it with my mind but it didn't work when I tried to move it with my hand it just passed through it.

Suddenly Elisa reminded me of the river I described in the dream and maybe it will help us travel through the river. I looked around and found a river flowing down hill. So I commanded the ball to move to the river and surprisingly it did so. It went downhill and drowned into the river when I and my friends reached the ball was fully gone under the river. We were standing there for sometime not knowing what to do and suddenly the part of the river where the orb has sunken started to boil and a jet of water shot upwards and while we were watching it happening three hands emerged from the river and pulled us into the water it was like running into a big wet sponge.

We were floating in the water and magically we were able to breathe. Then the water suddenly evaporated and we were dry again but we were now in a different place. When looked around we understood we were in front of the banyan tree I say in my dream. It was exactly like what I saw with a heap of roots covering something. But this time it was not reversing. The river I saw in the dream was not frozen ice. Evan came to me and asked whether this was the place I saw and I answered "Exactly like what I saw expect the fact that the river is frozen,"

Then I heard Elisa calling us to see something and what I saw send shiver up my bones. It was the same collection of skeletons that I saw in my dream but this time it was not throwing horns at me or attacking. We decided to not talk about it. Elisa started going through the book and stopped at a page and read. 'The true hero shall approach the tree and command it to back away and retrieve the sword but if he/she is not the one he and his companions shall disintegrate to bones.'

After hearing this I told them we had got our self into trouble. But they told it was the only chance we had on defeating demons. I wanted to finish this as soon as possible. After sometime I walked towards the ice river with them following me with their weapons ready even if I don't know why they need weapons to fight a tree, but I didn't ask. As I stepped on the ice thinking it will break. But it was solid enough for me to walk over. They stayed behind as the book said, only the hero shall approach. I didn't actually like being the main with all the attention, it made me uncomfortable. But this time I had no other option but to go on. As I walked into the garden I felt like I wanted to sleep right now but suddenly I felt conscious again. When I was near the heap of roots I kept my hand on it and closed my eyes. I concentrated on the image of the tree and commanded it to give me the sword. First noting happened but suddenly I felt like someone was tapping on my head with their fingers and when I opened my eyes I was felt like I was in a reversed time-lapse. I watched the tree becoming younger and younger while the roots were still there. The tree became a plant and the plant became a small sapling and all the roots suddenly started to go back and disappear into nothing and within moments I was standing in front of a sword with a silver handle and a white gem in the middle of the handle and the blade was struck into the ground and just standing near the blade makes me feel super vulnerable. When I looked back at the sapling. All the roots vanished and where there was a tree were now a clear ground and the sapling has vanished.

When I looked back at my friends they were standing with relief that we didn't die. When I put my hand on the handle suddenly I froze where I am standing, I mean I literally looked like a statue. Then I became normal and I tried to pull the sword out of the mud and when I did, I was holding a perfectly balanced and comfortable sword in my hand. But I didn't get much time to admire it , suddenly we started to float in the air and the floor beneath us started to became a black void and suddenly the white orb that led us here emerged from the water and it started shaking like something inside it was trying to escape and the next moment. It blasted and my vision went complete white.

I TRAIN FOR THE FIRST TIME

I woke up in the infirmary with Evan and Elisa near me. When they saw I was awake they came to me.

Oh, god you are ok. Both of them said in a worried voice at the same time.

When I asked them what happened they explained to me that we teleported near the river but I was unconscious so they took me to the infirmary. I was knocked out for almost two days.

So, what happened to the sword?

"Well we cannot find it. We looked all over the place and even the river but we didn't even find a piece." When Elisa said this there was a questioning in her voice.

Then suddenly the nurse came in and told them to get out and I could be discharged tonight and right now I needed rest. They looked at me once more like I was a patient about to die in the bed. I almost wanted to jump from the bed hit them for looking at me like that but I cannot blame them after I was knocked out for two days.

Just about an hour before dinner and entertainment The nurse came and told me I can go and also told me to not get knocked out while I am wet or else she will not let me in next time.

I went to my room and got freshened up. I was so upset because we took so much risk and went on this adventure and at last when we succeeded the sword was missing. When I was about to exit my room. I just thought it would be nice if the sword just appeared in my hand. And for my surprise it did. I suddenly felt a heaviness in my hand and when I looked it was the sword unharmed lying in my hand. I almost wanted to throw the sword out the window because my friends have been looking all over the place for the sword and it was in my gut the whole time.

The sword felt really balanced and comfortable in my hand like it was made for me. Its silver blade shined bright without any scratches or anything on it and its silver handle was very comfortable and in the intersection between the blade and the handle were a clear gem on one side and a black gem on the other side. The main part of the handle was made of soft leather. When I tried swinging it. It moved just like I wanted and I felt like it could read my mind. I willed it to disappear and it just vanished into silver particles. I thought at least it was not for nothing.

That night there was campfire and it was fun with dancing and music and other stuffs and after dinner as we were going to our rooms I called Evan and Elisa aside and showed them the sword and Elisa told she could punch me in the face cause they were worried all they did was for nothing and surprisingly Evan agreed too.

Dolof was nowhere to be seen and I think nobody else knows about where we went because nobody cared.

From the next day onwards I became pretty good at sword training but I couldn't keep going cause every dummy I touched either burnt up or got frozen in an ice cube or even sometimes just disappeared into dust. The rest of the time I had to narrate the whole story to the students and even teachers who came asking me about where I got my new sword. I ate in the mess hall for the first time. It was just a big room with many tables and chairs arranged in a zig-zag order and the plates and mugs kept refilling with whatever we wanted.

Cause of my sword problem with the dummies I had to practice with a normal sword which felt awkward after using the silver sword.

I tried everything like archery and other skills but I kept messing them up so I decided to mainly focus on swords while I also visited others once in a while. I also found out a very cool thing that my sword was not only a sword but it can morph into any weapon like Elisa had told me already but I forgot that.

I at last felt like normal kid after all and Evan, Elisa and I were now officially best friends and we were always together. We came to know about each other so much.

We had so much fun for about three weeks until Dolof finally returned and told us something that was not so pleasant.

THE CHILDHOOD OF A DEMON

When we were just relaxing on the garden bench. Suddenly a staff came to us and told us that Dolof had returned and he wants to meet us. We were a little surprised that he came back even if we were expecting him to. When we were walking towards his room the staff left us alone, so we had the space to discuss about where he would have been like he was tired of his job so he went for a three week long vacation in Hawaii or he just didn't want to be around if we failed the quest.

But when we saw him in his chair all our thoughts about him relaxing were busted. Sitting on the chair was a tired man who looked like didn't sleep for days and he had scratches on his hands and fore head and he looked like he didn't bath after playing with mud. Overall he looked the exact opposite of what he used to look like. We slowly walked to him because we were not sure if it was him because he didn't look anything like the smart and happy headmaster.

He looked like he would fall down any moment. He told us to sit down. His voice was not so good as well, now it sounded like he could barely speak. He went into a door nearby and said he would come back soon.

Five minutes passed......Ten minutes passed...... Twenty minutes passed........., I was kind of getting afraid he might have fell down somewhere. I told Evan and Elisa we should check if he was okay, they nodded and we started to standup but suddenly he came back. This time he was back to normal in his nice clothes and he was no more covered in dirt but he still had the weary looking expression on his face.

He sat in the chair in front of us. Elisa asked him if he was okay. There was real concern in her voice.

Yeah, yeah I am okay. If you are wondering where I was this whole time, I was out searching for information of the whereabouts of our demon friend.

Did you find anything? I asked almost wishing g he didn't because I was not ready yet.

Before I tell you that, have you done what I said?

You mean the sword?

Yes. Oh, we got it. I summoned the sword and showed him. He looked at it like it was a powerful thing which it was. I almost thought he would grab it from me and stab me right away but thankfully he didn't.

He tried to take it then he stopped as if remembering something.

Well, nice job three of you. I think now you would be ready for the net quest. The biggest one yet.

Evan interrupted. What are we talking about?

Well, I have found something about the where about of the demon. His lair is somewhere under water The Demon's sea. I think you should get started tomorrow itself, cause he knows about Eron's arrival here. He might try to attack the house soon.

This time I interrupted. What, if we go tomorrow and the house is attacked the damage will be huge. We can kill him when he comes to attack. That would be better.

Dolof's expression changed to a disappointed one. Well, I wish that was possible because he will not be able to be killed while his life source is safe.

'What? ' I didn't understand but from the looks on Evan's and Elisa's face I think they understood.

Well I am sure you don't know. Dolof started explaining. Well Tyrone is the most powerful demon that we have faced as we know and he became so powerful that he had the power to extract his life from himself and keep it safe somewhere else while he can still go around killing people. So whatever we do will not affect he as long as his life source is UN harmed. Even if we destroy his life source we will have to kill him because it will only destroy his immortality.

Ok that explains it. So what is the plan exactly? We go to his lair and ask him to hand over his life to us or else we will eat his ice cream?

All three of them managed a little smile.

Dolof shook his head. No, we will not black mail him with ice cream, we will have to trespass into his territory and find where he keeps his life source. We will have to release his life source into his own body so we will be able to destroy it when we fight him. But I believe it will not be an easy task.

'Sounds dangerous. ' I told them and they agreed.

Well there is one more thing that you all need to know. When Dolof said this there was a sad expression on his face.

Tyrone was also a student of Saftor but he turned out to be evil.

I believe it is time you go to your rooms and your food will be delivered to your rooms. You should start packing and should also get rest because you have a big day ahead.

We stood up and said good night to Dolof and started walking to our rooms. We were discussing about our plans about tomorrow but when we reached our rooms we decided to not waste anymore time. We decided to discuss about the plans tomorrow morning.

I got into my room and looked for a back pack and fond a good one in the cupboard. I filled it with some dress and I realized it had unlimited storage, no matter how much I jeep in it doesn't fill. So I decided to put in some more clothes and some food just in case of emergency and some huge water bottles cause I am pretty sure we will not be having fresh water elsewhere. Then I got a sudden thought about the weight of the bag because I have filled it with pretty heavy items so it should be pretty heavy. But when I tried on the backpack it felt as if it had nothing in it.

Then I got freshened up and when I returned there was a food trolley so I ate some food and went to sleep at seven o'clock.

Operation: I don't know

    I woke up at four o'clock because I have already slept nine hours. I thought Evan and Elisa should be already awake because they usually woke me up sometimes. So I exited my room to look if they were awake. I knocked on Evan's door but nobody answered, so I went inside and to be true I think his room is better than mine but in a different way. His room was like an old style cottage with shelves decorated with swords, action figures and some books. His room didn't have many items. One cupboard was in the corner and a window near it with a beautiful view towards the training ground.

    On a normal bed in the corner was lying Evan with no movement. So I decided to get out. I was pretty sure at least Elisa was wake because she said about making plans at early morning. So I knocked on her door but still no response. So I went inside and her room was just like a resort room but she was also asleep on her bed.

    So I exited from there also and I decided to go freshen up anyway. After I freshened up I put on a plain black t-shirt which felt comfortable at the moment and I also put on black pants. It didn't go with my blue hair and eyes so I thought of myself with black hair and eyes and it worked. I haven't tried that for weeks but now I looked better.

I decided to go wake Evan and Elisa so I knocked on the door but thankfully this time they were both awake and I told them to meet me at the library (which was open at this time because Dolof told the staffs to keep it open so that we could look for important information.) I simply told them to wear plain black dress for you know like uniforms. (I don't know why I said that but it just felt right to say.)\

Just for you to know that here the sun came up at five o'clock, don't ask me why because I don't know. After taking my bag and thinking if I would return to my room alive again I went to the library which was open. I went to the biggest table because we were going to take so many books. Within a few minutes Evan and Elisa also came. Both of them had bags which looked similar to mine but was different colors. Mine was black, Evan's was grey and Elisa's was brown. They were also wearing black dress like I asked them so if we stand together people are obviously going to call us the three demons.

I greeted them good morning and they greeted back. As soon as we sat down Elisa started saying the plan.

'We are first going to need a water travel, after that is set we have to somehow travel to the Demon's lake where no one is said to come back from and we need to find his lair under water, then we will have to fight the world's most dangerous monsters and somehow find that life source and return it to Tyrone so that we can kill him. Sounds easy. '

So how are we going to do this exactly?

Elisa leaned over to the table and started speaking.

"There is more we need to do. First we have to travel to the mount Delf which is hundreds of miles from here and once we get there we need to find the flower of the Ackiles which will protect us from the cursed water of the Demon's sea, then we have to extract the essence of the flower and make a potion from it, then we have to go to the Demon's lake and fight the monsters and get the life source, then we have to fight the demon himself. "

What exactly is this flower of Ackiles? I asked her

Elisa looked at me and continued. In the ancient times Demons didn't have any personal territory so they were always vulnerable. So all the demons of that time put their powers together and made the Demon's Sea or in its real name The Grakius. This sea is endless and the water in this sea was cursed by the demons to keep out the nice people.

So where does this Flower of Ackiles come.

"From the creation of world there are some godly beings who look like humans but are way more than that, they were called 'The Ackiles. ' They were created for one single purpose, to clear they ways of heroes and good people. When they came to know about this sea they created a new type of flower and blessed it with the ability to protect its consumer from the curses of the sea water and they couldn't make it too common because it was only for much needed purposes. So they planted it on mount Delf and even if we get there we need to do challenges to prove us worthy. "

'So, we have a rough time ahead. Well before its assembly time we better go to Dolof and present our plan. ' I suggested.

So, we exited the library after returning the books to where they belong and took our bag and went to Dolof's office.

I DRINK ONE MORE POTION

When we got to the office Dolof was already there talking to our potion master who obviously teaches us about potions in the MI or Magical Items class. He wore a black cloak with the designs of different colored potions in bottles all over it; he had a box in front of him placed on Dolof's table.

When Dolof saw us he told the master something and the master exited the room but left the box there itself. We went near Dolof and told him our plan, once we were done he smiled and said

'Well, there you go. I was about to inform you about the flower but it looks like you have already found out. But anyway I don't see how you would get there soon enough. '

Elisa who was presenting the plan got a little uncomfortable when he asked the question but Evan told Dolof that we were going to ask him about that. Dolof looked like he was totally expecting it. "I think, you are in the right place. I asked our respected potion master to make three bottle of teleportation juice for you which will take you to the neighborhood of mount Delf." He pointed at the box which I totally forgot about, inside it was three round potion bottles containing shiny pink liquid which I suddenly realized, was the same potion I drank which brought me here but just pink color. Just looking at it made I want to grab one and drink it right away. Then a question struck me. " How long do we have before Tyrone attacks? "

When I asked this Dolof's expression darkened like he didn't actually want to share the information but he had no choice. ' Within this week so you have to hurry. Don't ask me more about it. '

We were about to ask him more but we decided not to and hurry up. " So shall we now go and eat our breakfast ? "

" Yes, just keep your bag and other items here. After breakfast come here and you shall start your journey."

When we went to the mess hall there was only one table with three chairs and plates filled with food. We ate without speaking much, probably we were all thinking about how to speed up the quest as much as possible in their own way.

After we were done we went to the office but no one was there, so we decided not to bother anyone. We took our luggage and took one potion from the box and uncapped it. Its smell was so good I wanted to drink it instantly but we decided to drink at the same time.

" To defeating Tyrone. " I raised my drink and the others followed. And we drank it at the same time. I felt like my head was spinning and I would fall any moment and suddenly my vision went black and I couldn't feel my body.

When I could feel my body again and regained my vision back. I was lying on lush green grass with flowers around me. On my both sides were Evan and Elisa regaining consciousness slowly. Maybe I was able to recover soon because it was my second time doing this.

When all three of us were fully ok we looked around and there was nothing expects one giant hill and plain green grass and flowers everywhere else. Suddenly I heard wings flapping and when I looked around both of my friends were looking at the mountain. When I looked what they were looking, I found six or seven people coming down the mountain expect the fact that they had black wings.

I BATTLE MY FIRST MONSTER.

They were wearing Battle armor and some of them had spears, others had swords, they were normal humans but had black wings. When they landed near us their wings dissolved into black particles.

They came in a V formation with three people on each side of one, that one person looked like their leader who was holding some kind of staff with the tiny statue of a woman flying with wings. The whole things gold. They came near and their leader ordered the others to stay behind and she came forward. " I am Zelda the supreme Ackile. What is the purpose of your visit to Mount Delf ? "

For a moment none of us could speak then Evan came forward and started explaining about our quest and about us wanting the flower. After hearing he Zelda told her assistants something and then they came towards us and each two of them grabbed one of our hands and suddenly they started glowing and had to close my eyes from bursting. When the Glow died I was standing with Evan Elisa on my each side and when I took a quick look around I understood we were in the battle ground of and arena. The arena was not too big but also not small. All around us on stone benches were hundreds of Ackiles shouting. One the other end of the ground was a cell with growling coming from it and just above the cell on the gallery was one raised platform with two chairs on it and the person sitting on one of them was Zelda and on the other was a tall and good looking guy who was like twenty or something. Zelda stood from her chair and raised her hand as if to shut the crowd. She started speaking in so loud that us standing about forty or fifty meters away from her cam clearly hear her. " My fellow friends today we are going to do another battle to see if our guests are worthy for what they are asking. We hadn't had one of these for so long that it was almost forgotten. Today they shall fight the dangerous beast that we were unfortunately unable to destroy. " There was a loud shouting when she said the last part.

When Elisa heard the we-were-unable-to-destroy part her face became filled with fear. When Zelda had finished speaking Elisa came forward and started asking Zelda " How are we able to destroy the monster, which was unable to be defeated by godly and powerful beings like you ? " When she asked this the whole crowd started protesting as if she had slapped each of them on their face. Zelda ordered them to shut up and she turned towards us with a forced smile on her face.

" Oh dear we accept that we are godly beings and we are quite powerful but there are way more greater powers in the universe whose powers are infinitely more powerful than ours, and this is also applicable to the bad side. There are monsters and bad people whose powers are greater than ours. And just for your information we are not as powerful as you have heard. They are just legends written by people who haven't even seen us in person. The only reason we are able to keep this monster under control until the right person who is destined to kill this beast is with of the help of other greater powers. Now if you might keep the rest of your doubts to yourself, we shall start the battle. "

My hands were shivering after hearing about the monster which we are about to fight, who was unable to be defeated by the powerful Ackiles. If there are greater powers in the universe, which are more powerful than people who can create the cure to cursed water and stuffs, I don't want them, to be on the bad side.

If somehow we were not the ones destined to kill this beast, would we be its breakfast or will we be saved just before our death. I kept the questions aside and concentrated on how to defeat the monster.

When I summoned my sword there was a loud gasp in the crowd and even Zelda and the guy next to her seemed to be surprised. The guy next to Zelda announced. " This boy bears the sacred sword, this is going to be an epic battle." There was a loud cheer in the crowd. The guy snapped his fingers and the bars of the cell dissolved into sand.

I thought it would be a good idea to slow down the monster before we could attack it, so I willed my sword to change into a magical chain. The sword glowed bright white and when the glow did I was hold a five meter long silver chain in my hand which I figured out would expand according to my will.

Suddenly there was a loud growl and something shot out from the cage. The moment I saw it I wanted to say we don't need the flower we are leaving. I am pretty sure you would have fainted at the sight of this thing if you were alone.

The thing was as big as a mini truck. It was like a monster took from a horror movie. I had blood red skin and a face between a dogs's and bats. It had two big fully black eyes. Its teeth were like a lion's and it had dragon's legs but smaller. When it comes near there is a smell of flesh and blood.

When it saw my chain. It backed away as it radiated power that was not so good for it.

" You want some? Okay " I tried to throw the chain around its neck and the chain expanded on its own as if already knowing what to do. But the monster was fast and I missed the shot. The chain shrank itself. The monster was surrounded Evan, Elisa and me. They were trying to get the monster's attention. One look from both of them and I understood the plan. Evan threw his sword at it and the monster turned to his direction, it was slowly advancing as if it was in no hurry. I took the chance and threw the chain around its neck and this time it was perfect shot. The chain made two or three rounds on its neck and where the chain had touched it, smoke began to form as if the skin was burning under the chair. The monster wailed in pain and started shaking and running around. It was no problem for me because the chain kept expanding and shrinking as the monster ran away or shook. In between my friends kept stabbing and hitting it. After minutes of running and shaking. The monster slowed down as if it was tired. There was a loud cheer from the crowd.

The monster's eyes were now grey. It was trying hard to keep itself from falling. When I became sure that the monster wasn't moving. I willed the chain to become a sword again. Which was not a genius move. My friends were also tired from running and fighting. Suddenly the monster became conscious again and charge at me. Which was also a not so genius move. When it was close enough I pointed the sword towards the monsters face and it disintegrated into dust. There whole crowd stood up and cheered but some looked disappointed cause there will be no more such battle or test or whatever. I ran towards my friends who were leaning against the wall.

" Are you okay ?"

" Expect the fact that we just fought a deadly monster, we are okay."

Zelda came down towards us. " Well done, warriors you have proven yourself worthy."

I asked her " Where is the flower that you promised ? "

' You will be given as I promised, you people look so tired. Why don't you rest while the potion is being made.'

When I looked at my tired friends I felt bad for pulling them into such trouble. " We could use some rest and food. "

' Follow me.' Zelda walked towards a solid wall near us but when she came near the wall into shaped into an entrance.

WE BECOME THE VIPS

When we entered the entrance closed and became a solid wall but I didn't have time to think if it was a trap. So we followed her into a big corridor like inside a palace. From the roof hung many bright lamps and the walls were made of marble and a designed carpet was laid all over the floor. We followed her into another corridor but this one was not everlasting. It stopped within ten or so meters and on each wall was a door.

Zelda led Evan and Elisa to the rooms on the side and led me to the last room. When I entered I was so relived and tired that I wanted to fall down where I was standing and sleep there it. The room was air conditioned and there was a big four poster bed and there was a door which must be the entrance to the storage. My backpack was already on my bed.

I went to my luggage took out a pair of clothes and went to the bathroom which was also super luxury. After than I put my bad clothes in the backpack and tried to sleep. As soon as I lay on the bed I slept. When I woke up no one was there. I washed my face and I felt as good as new. I took my bag and went to wake up my friends because we need to complete the quest ASAP. But then I realized I was the late person. There was a door open in the corridor we first came through and I could see Elisa and Evan sitting on a chair and eating with their backpack near the table. I went there and found out that they were eating with Zelda and The mysterious Guy who would be the male head Ackile. I went to them and when the head boy saw me he said "At last the sleepy head has wakened, come sit and eat your last meal before you depart." I wanted to hit the man in the face but when I saw the food I couldn't do anything expect sit down and eat, because I was so hungry.

I sat near my friends and they greeted me and I did greet them back. The whole table was filled with different types of food and drinks. I ate as much as my stomach can hold and when we were finished. The plates and everything disappeared. When we came back from washing our hands the head boy and head girl were sitting on the other end of the table as if they wanted to talk to us. We sat down near them. Zelda started speaking. " Well we can't just give you some potions only for helping us to remove one of our big headaches, so we decided to gift each of you something special. " She looked at Elisa " You look like the navigator of this group, so I give you this." She took something from her pocket and gave it to her. It was an old style pocket watch locket with a chain. It looked normal expect that it had caps on each side. "This will guide you to your destination and you can also get the navigation to any places that you ask it expect some places which are heavily protected with magic. " Elisa looked at it like it was the most valuable thing she had ever seen. She opened on side of the watch and it was a watch itself and nothing special. " It shows the time of the place which you wish. But don't worry it doesn't have any limit." Zelda added. The watch face was complicated but Elisa seemed to understand. She said the watch to show the time and date at Saftor. When she saw the date she almost forgot how to breathe. The hands of the watch spun fast and rested on eight am. But she was looking at the section of date. It was written eleventh June. I couldn't believe it. It is our fourth day after we started the quest. Evan also seemed to notice he was staring at the Watch piece. I asked Zelda if the machine is damaged.

She laughed " No dear, the thing is. The territory of Ackiles and our territory were only added to the timeline after three days of the creation of the universe so we are always three days backwards. If you spend one day here, you will be spending four days in the normal place. Even thinking about it makes my head burst, it is so complicated but I have said what you need to know." Just for your information. The watch has other features also.

' What features, exactly ? '

" What is the fun if I tell you everything, find the answer on your own. "

Elisa opened the other side and it was a compass but made of different shades of gold. It was pointing to our right side and it only had one needle.

The Head Guy turned towards Evan and gave him a wicked smile which I thought would be his only superpower. He took out something from his pocket and handed it over to Evan. It was another locket but this time it was just a round piece of gold and nothing special. The piece of gold looked heavy. The guy started speaking. " This will provide you transportation whenever you want and it has no limit and you can change it you whatever vehicle you want, and importantly don't try it here or else I will take it back." Evan took it from his hand and put it on his neck as if he had seen it enough or was scared that it would turn into a truck in the dining room.

Now both of them turned towards me. But before they could say anything I started speaking. " Please, don't give me a locket I already have one. " I showed them my Locket which was a nine pointed star with a purple gem in the middle. I haven't shown this to anyone because I had a bad feeling it was something special.

Zelda and the guy stared at it like it was the end of a gun pointing at their head. They looked at each other, thankfully instead of acting weird they became normal again. My friends seemed dot is busy with their own gifts so they didn't even look. I put the locket back inside my shirt and decided not to find out its secret cause I don't want to know.

Zelda was the first one to speak. "Don't, fear we are not giving you any locket. " Her sound felt like she was forcing the words and she felt very scared even if I don't know if they were allowed to be afraid of a single locket but I decided not to ask.

She continued. " You look like you need to know much more about the magical world and I also think you are pretty good with modern electronics. So I give you something that will help you understand the magical world. " She stood up from her chair and went to a room nearby and the head guy also followed. After few minutes she came back but the guy didn't. She held something black in her hand. She came near and gave it to me. I realized it was a smart watch. Zelda explained that I will find infinite knowledge in this some very useful features or items other than knowledge which could save my life. And she also said that she cannot explain how cause she was not so good with machines so I have to figure it out.

I was actually happy because I really wanted an easy way to know about the things happening around so it will be very helpful. I thanked her and she told me I deserved me and I really needed it. I was a little embarrassed cause I know very little compared to others. Then when all of us were done admiring our presents.

A minor Ackile came from the corridor holding a box with something in it. She said something to her leader aka Zelda and handed over the box to her. Zelda looked at us and said 'now the main part.' She took out two vials containing white milky liquid from the box and handed it over to Evan and Elisa. She kept the box aside and looked at us. My friends were looking at me. I asked here where is mine.

She smiled and asked me " Have you really retrieve the sacred sword from the tree of protection ? "

' Yes I retrieved it and my friends also came along to help me. '

She smiled again and looked at Elisa as if she knew the answer. Elisa thought for some time and looked at Zelda and me. She made a surprised face.

" How could have I forgotten it, Eron your sacred sword was blessed by many powers and one of the blessings is from the Ackiles that means you don't need the potion to survive the cursed water."

' What, couldn't you have told me this earlier.'

' Oops, sorry I forgot.'

Zelda interrupted. ' So I think it is time for you to leave. You only have four days including today to save you house. '

None of us protested, we took our bag and followed Zelda towards the mountain where we came from. When we got to the top of the mountain she turned towards us and told 'Farewell my little heroes, you shall be on your own way from now onwards. ' After saying this she disappeared into golden light.

Evan looked at us excitedly and told us it's time to check out his new gift. He pulled the locket and it came loose from the chain without any problem like it was magnetically attached to it. Evan added the fact that it was very heavy when holding and very light when wearing as a locket. He threw the piece of gold on the ground and willed it to become a caravan and it did. The gold started shining and a medium sized white colored caravan with golden stripes here and there started loading like it was some three-d art. Within a few moments we were standing near a real caravan.

All three of us said " Cool " at the same time.

THE RUNNING, FLYING AND SWIMMING CARAVAN

We entered the Caravan and understood that it was just like our Unlimited storage back pack. Inside the caravan it was a replica of the castle. Then Evan wondered if it will change to whatever theme if we set it so. He went to the driver's compartment where you would expect steering wheel and many switches and all but all there was a few switches a seat with a manual book lying on it.

We left Evan to study the manual. When we were about to enter our rooms, the whole replica changed to the theme of our rooms in Saftor. We looked at Evan who was pressing his hand on a switch and was grinning at us. We told him this would be better and we went to our rooms. It was just like the original rooms. We went in and kept our bags on the beds and went to Evan to find out how to work this thing. We didn't think about how or who will drive this thing because just before we left the head guy came to say us farewell and he also told Evan that his vehicles has autopilot which was a great relief cause none of us don't know how to drive.

We spent about a couple of hours going through the whole manual and found so many interesting things like there is an option to play music and turn on the disco ball and some of the most helpful ones we found were that there is an inbuilt unlimited food supply, but the main one is that it supports any type of navigation Devices which means Elisa's Locket will be able to be used without someone always looking at it. She tried to pull the locket and it also came out from the chain without any struggle like It was magnet. When She held it near an empty place near the switches it flew to the surface like it was two magnets. Nothing happened until she told it to navigate the way towards Demon's sea and the compass needle started to spin like crazy When it stopped it was no more a traditional compass, it was a digital screen showing a text written ' Destination: Demon's sea' suddenly the vehicle started on its own and another digital screen popped out where the driver's wheel should have been. It showed an option to start the journey and Evan without hesitating, clicked it and the caravan started moving and took many turns here and there and it was at last it came to the edge of a cliff and it didn't stop it increased its speed and Evan was trying to stop it with pressing random buttons but nothing worked and the caravan was no longer touching the ground, we grabbed the nearest thing we can find tried not to scream or fall down but there was no need cause the caravan was flying. Suddenly on the screen popped up a 3-d model of the caravan which was no longer a caravan it was a small airplane.

I and Elisa suddenly realized that we were holding hands and we let it go.

The idea of the caravan being a small airplane was both good and bad as well. The good thing we didn't fall to our death after going through this much and the bad side, with this Evan started his pilot speech. " Ladies and Gentle men, welcome to Evan airplane services. Please make yourself comfortable throughout your flight from The mystical Mount Delf to you death in Demon's sea."

We went back to our rooms but we cannot rest because we had more than enough rest in the palace so I decided to go through the watch that Zelda gave me. There were many items in it but I was not in the mood to study so I kept going through for some time until there was a small shaking and when I went to see what happened the airplane which was previously a Caravan was now a Mini cruise and now we were on sea. Now I was seriously jealous and I felt that Elisa would have felt the same way but there was something that told me that our gifts were way more important and powerful.

WE GO FOR THE SWIM

We were traveling for so long that even Evan who was trying out everything in the boat or plane or whatever got bored. After what felt like a day. We found something interesting. A piranha without eyes and with blood stained teeth.

When we were looking for more dangerous creatures, the cruise suddenly hit an invisible barrier and we almost fell of the deck cause of the force. The barrier seemed to alert the monsters because there was a huge wave of different types of monsters coming from a distance.

Evan ran inside and started to control the boat to go to the nearest shore which was visible to our right. When we got to the shore we noticed that the monsters cannot come closer because of the barrier. I am Elisa got out of the ship with our luggage and Evan Pressed some button on the control panel and the whole boat shrunk to a single gold coin and next to it was Elisa's compass/watch. We didn't even needed to pick them up because they flew automatically came back to the locket and I understood it was all magic tricks.

It was becoming very dark, so we decided to camp for the night. We all packed a portable tent which we found on the caravan. And we ran into a problem, that is doing know how to put up a tent. So I decided to look in the watch if there is anything and then I found out its special power. It will do it for you. When I accidently clicked on an option, the screen of the watch slid the both sides like a camera shutter and some white ghosts came from the watch and put up the three tents perfectly and went back in, while they were working I was standing there in horror. Believe me, it is not fun to watch ghosts oozing out of your watch while you are wearing it.

And we might have found the super power of Elisa's watch/compass also. She was just going through it in her tent and she accidently found one of the secret switches. When she pressed it the screen showed a clock face showing six o'clock in the morning and it was written on the edge. ' This would be a great time to simply go for a swim in the water of deaths. ' When she came to show us we didn't understand at first, then we understood that it had the power to show the perfect time to do something and it showed six in the morning cause the monsters are less powerful when the sun starts rising.

As she was always the early waking person, she told us she would wake us at five in the morning.

We went to our tents and just laid there realizing that it might be the last sleep that we will wake from.

I decided to keep all my thoughts aside and sleep peacefully.

I partly expected monsters to attack us at the night, so if Elisa didn't say that it was her, I might have attacked her. It was still dark and humid but when I remembered about what we needed to do, I woke up fast.

Remark: ' First of all, I know there have been many scenes with me crying and being lazy and upset but mark my words, you will be doing the same if you were in my stage fighting monsters and realizing about your real parents and all that stuff. So let's continue. '

When I exited my tent it was still pitch black and the only light came from the portable lamp we had bought with us and the moon was nowhere to be seen. The facts about sun, moon and the sky in this place just don't make any sense because Dolof had already told me several times that we were not even on a planet.

I went near the water and when I was about to wash my face I heard Evan shouting at me about what I am doing. HE asked that if I had a desire to burn my face with the cursed water. But when I gave him the did-you-forgot face he stopped.

I still wondered what all can I and my sword do. I went to see if there is anything useful that we can take while we are running towards our death but I found nothing and I wondered if my watch is water proof but I didn't want to find it the hard way, so I left it in my bag. If we use a submarine to go down there we doubted it would survive, so Evan willed his locket to become the caravan again and we tossed our bags inside and he had his locket back and we were ready to die. They drank the potion and said they feel kind of different.

When the clock hit six we started. Evan bought a automatic inflating raft to go to a deep part of the sea so we have a good idea. He threw it on the ground and it suddenly became a raft and so we started. When we thought it was deep enough we decided to jump, but before we could jump, the raft explode because we forgot that this was no normal sea water. We fell into the water and somehow magically we were able to breathe and talk underwater just like on land which we realized was the power of the potion or the blessing. We couldn't see anything because the water below us was dark.

I summoned the sword and they took out their weapons and we started swimming to the bottom. When the vision began to become clear we regretted going on this quest. All over the sea floor were castles made of black stones and others. It was like a full kingdom under the sea. Many monsters were swimming here and there but none of them seem to notice us.

All the castles were starting to get destroyed expect one. It had a white ball shining inside it and there were no monsters or animals near it, so we decided o take our chance and leave. We swam slowly towards the castle so no monsters see us. When we were near it. It was like some force trying to push us away.

I was getting suspicious about the life source. It just feels too easy. I used all my strength and went towards it and when I put my hand on it , the force stopped. I took it in my hands and it felt like air. I asked my friends, if they are sure it is the right one. Elisa replied. ' I don't know, it is the only thing we can find here.' But Evan's reply was strange. ' I think it is the right one. Don't ask me how but I can feel life in it.' We stared at him but chose not to ask. When we were about to leave, all the buildings started to rumble and slowly fall down. We shot up wards but before we reached the surface. Something grabbed our legs. I expected monsters. But it was the hands similar to the one we summoned in the river. It pulled us downwards to the ground. I held the life source tight, cause I feared it might slip from my hand.

Suddenly we were on land. Near the river outside Saftor. I was still holding the life source. I couldn't think of anything else expect, retrieving this thing was too easy to be true. I stood there thinking about it. But suddenly my friends came and told me to come fast and they showed me that smoke was rising from the forest on the other side and I instantly knew that Tyrone was attacking and we needed to hurry, so we sprinted up the hill.

WE DEFEATED A DEMON TOO EASILY

All the way up I cannot stop thinking we were going to do something wrong. I snapped back to reality when my friends screamed ' Oh My God 'they were looking at the same figure I saw in my dream it was holding the same sword. He had many cracks in his body which was made of black stone and through the cracks you can see blue fire burning inside him.

He was alone but I had the feeling that a huge army is on its way. When we got near the forest all children and staffs and security and even Dolof was standing there. Everyone expect Dolof was armed with different weapons like spears, bows, swords, etc....

The demon was standing in front of the army looking down at them. He smiled wickedly and started speaking in the same voice. ' Well where is your little hero. Let me see him and kill him. I might spare you.' Dolof replied ' You are not killing anyone. '

' Well brave little old man, you haven't changed, have you ? Still stubborn and protective. Then you sentenced yourself and your little lovely children to death.'

He backed up a little bit and started creating a blue projectile between his hands. But he suddenly stopped when he saw us.

We ran towards him from the other side and looked up at him. ' He is right, you are not going to kill anyone. ' When I raised the life source I couldn't see whether his expression was surprised or happiness.

It floated upwards and shot at his chest. He began to fall down but he started to turn to black fog and he shrank in size. And when the fog has disappeared. Lying where the demon was a boy about my age and he was unconscious. We ran towards him. I was a little shocked. The demon didn't attack us at all instead he turned into a little boy ?

The boy suddenly choked out blue fire which could have almost burned Elisa's face if she hadn't move in time. He slowly regained consciousness. We kept our sword ready.

The boy looked weak , very weak. He wore the dress which looked exactly like the one Dolof had worn most of the time. I told my friends that we should help him. First they hesitated but then they helped me to take him and lean him to a nearby tree. He slowly started regaining full consciousness.

Once he had enough energy to open his eyes. We asked him who he was. He still looked very weak but he tried to speak.

' I…. I..am…… I am '

Before he could finish someone behind us said " Henry " When we looked it was Dolof. We didn't realize he was standing behind us. But what surprised me was that he had tears down his chin. We were speechless. We haven't ever seen him crying.

He knelt in front of the boy. "Henry, you... you are alive."

The boy looked at him and said ' Dolof ? '

We were once again speechless. Dolof wiped his tears and looked up where the army of children was. But now there was only a staff standing there. Dolof shouted at him to bring the medicals down here. After a few minutes the medics came down and took Henry with them probably to the infirmary.

Before we could speak, when The medics were half the hill carrying him. Black fog shot out of his mouth but the medics didn't seem to notice they were busy struggling to take him up the hill.

The black fog came towards us and floated in the air and suddenly it expanded to the size of a Big TV screen and it showed a fogy figure with blue burning eyes that I guessed was Tyrone. He turned towards us and started speaking in a more terrifying and less humanlike voice.

" I just thought you should know the answer to your question about the quest being so easy you know. Actually I wanted you to find the life source which kept my demonic soul linked to the puny Henry boy's body. Now I have enough power to make myself a body but the life source overpowered me and I was unable to free myself from his body. So I wanted a mortal like you to do that for me. I think your question is answered and we shall meet again at your death. " The foggy TV disappeared.

We watched it in horror. It explained it all We just freed Tyrone from Henry's body which kept him from using his full powers and now that he is free, we are doomed.' I turned towards my friends and they Were also shocked. But Dolof was standing there as if he expected this to happen.

He looked at me and my friends and told us that we had done a nice job and now we can go back to our rooms. We tried to ask him questions but he went away without saying anymore.

WE GET A NEW BOY IN OUR TRIO

We sat in my room regretting what we just did but then we concluded that if we tried to kill Tyrone in Henry's body, Henry will die and Tyrone will be free anyway so we just saved a precious life.

It has been about couple of hours so we decided to go see the Henry boy. We reached the infirmary and when we asked the nurse if we could enter, she allowed which was unusual. When we got near him we saw Dolof talking with him. When he saw us, he told Henry something and stood up from the chair he was sitting on and turned towards us ' Well, I think you have many doubts especially about him, but I can't explain or say anything. You can ask Henry himself, but don't take it too far. ' Before we could say anything, he left. So we decided to sit near him.

' So you are Henry ? ' Elisa asked.

He looked in a way better mood. He smiled and said ' Yes I am Henry. '

We all introduced ourselves. Evan asked him ' So who are you exactly and what happened ? ' When he heard this question his smile faded slowly and his expression looked like remembering a bad memory.

" I am Henry Cabellan. I was just a normal Palin boy and one day I got the chance here like you people and I stayed here. By that time some demon attacked my hometown and killed my parents. When I went to the wreckage there was nothing left but when I was on my way back from that place I felt like something different but I didn't give it any thinking cause I had just lost my parents. But after a few day I started to have dreams about some foggy figure in my head and suddenly one day I got fully possessed by Tyrone and from that day to now I don't know anything. Expect that people now recognize me as Tyrone and nobody recognizes me as Henry expect Dolof. "

Evan was not quite expecting a big speech. ' Oh that answers my questions.'

I felt really sorry for him.

I asked him ' Don't you have any friends ? '

' No, I was born decades ago and I had no friends here cause everyone thought I was weird. '

The born-decades-ago part made me think very hard but then I left it in my think-at –free-time list.

I gave him a little smile and said. ' Same, I also don't have much friends expect these two. You can be our friend if you are interested.

You kidding me? , I am in.

ERON AND FRIENDS
WILL RETURN.

Made in the USA
Columbia, SC
25 August 2022

65308799R00070